Ellie Ultra is published by Stone Arch Books,
A Capstone Imprint
1710 Roe Crest Drive
North Mankato, Minnesota 56003
www.mycapstone.com

Text © 2017 Gina Bellisario
Illustrations © 2017 Stone Arch Books

Library of Congress Cataloging-in-Publication Data is
available on the Library of Congress website.

ISBN: 978-1-4965-3142-1 (hardcover) — 978-1-4965-3146-9
(paperback) — 978-1-4965-3150-6 (ebook PDF)

Summary: Ellie is bored and decides to bring her favorite
stuffed animal, Super Fluffy, to life to keep her company.
But when she accidentally brings the super-villain
Doomsday to life too, Super Fluffy needs to do more than
help Ellie fight boredom — they have to save the city!

Editor: Alison Deering
Designer: Hilary Wacholz

Printed in Canada.
010033S17

For Sofia and Milla, my heroes — love, Mom

Super Fluffy
to the Rescue

written by Gina Bellisario

illustrated by Jessika von Innerebner

STONE ARCH BOOKS
a capstone imprint

TABLE OF CONTENTS

CHAPTER 1

Saturdoom

It was just another day in the city of Winkopolis. Kitties mewed. Birds chirped. Joggers jogged. Everyone was doing the same old, ordinary things. Everyone, mind you, but the girl who lived at 8 Louise Lane.

That girl was Ellie Ultra. She was playing Go Fish, a very ordinary card game, but she was picking cards faster than a racehorse on turbocharged roller skates. It was *extra*ordinary.

"Woo-hoo! I won!" Ellie cheered. Rocket-fast, she whipped down one, then two, then three pairs of cards. Her hands were empty in a flash. "Beat you again, Cyclops."

Cyclops, the Ultras' giant, one-eyed iguana, looked mad — probably because he had also lost at Crazy Eights and Old Maid. He snatched his *Lizard's Life* magazine, slunk off the chair, and disappeared.

Ellie slumped in her seat. The iguana wasn't much competition, but at least he was someone to play with. All of Ellie's non-lizard friends were busy, and she was bored with a capital *B*.

After Ellie put away the cards, her chin fell into her hand. "Saturday? More like Saturdoom," she said sadly. "I'm doomed to spend the whole day alone."

More than bored, Ellie was lonely. Being a superhero, she had faced the world's worst villains, including Captain Blob and the Goo Crew, and Queen Bee. But loneliness? It was the worst!

Loneliness blurred Ellie's X-ray vision. It turned her super strength into cooked spaghetti. She couldn't even fly. Loneliness made her sink like a stone in a tub of toxic waste.

"I wouldn't be lonely if I had a sidekick," Ellie muttered. Then it hit her. "Wait a super second!"

She glanced at her watch. All was not lost! It was three o'clock, which meant that Hannah — Ellie's better-than-a-sidekick best friend — would be done with dance class.

Ellie knew she was powerless to beat loneliness all by her lonesome. But if she teamed up with Hannah, she could sock that feeling with a one-two punch!

Crossing her fingers, Ellie dialed Hannah's number. Hopefully, Hannah could help save the day.

"Hello?" Hannah answered.

"Hi!" Ellie squealed. "Do you want to come over? I can teach you how to play Guess That Super-Villain. It's the best game ever!"

Hannah sighed loudly. Uh-oh. It sounded like Super Bestie was in trouble! "I wish I could," she replied, "but I'm stuck helping my mom. It's for Cece."

Now it was Ellie's turn to sigh. Cece was Hannah's little sister. Sometimes, Hannah had to do things for her, like carry her backpack or tie her shoes. "What do you have to do?" Ellie asked.

"Her birthday party is tomorrow. It's at our house, so my mom wants help setting everything up."

Ellie's heart sank. Hannah's mom had unleashed the terrible forces of Choredom. Even Ellie was powerless to stop them!

"That stinks," she said.

"I know," Hannah agreed. "It's a princess party, so my mom's going crown-cuckoo. She's turning our backyard into Tiara Land. We'll have games, fancy finger sandwiches, and even a bouncy castle. I have to glue gems on the crown party favors."

Hannah sighed again, louder this time. "Hey, if you're not fighting super-villains, why don't you come to the party? You can help with the dragon piñata."

Ellie was a super fan of princesses, especially Princess Power, the comic book superhero of Sparkle Kingdom. But she would rather face Princess Power's archenemy, the Troll King, than pint-sized candy fiends.

"Um, I'll have to wait and see," she said. "You never know when a super-villain might strike."

"Okay," Hannah replied. "Well, I better get started on those crowns. Hope to see you tomorrow! Bye!"

"Bye." Ellie hung up the phone. She felt a little sorry for Hannah. Loneliness you could fight. But chores? Never!

With Hannah unable to play, all hope seemed lost. It reminded Ellie of the time she'd been caught by Bubble Trouble. That villain had used his Gum Ray — with extra-chewy power — to snag her. Luckily, she'd had a trick up her cape — peanut butter! After unsticking her curls, Ellie had nabbed him instead.

She'd had her parents to thank for getting her out of that sticky situation. Maybe they could lift her lonely spirits!

Ellie raced downstairs to the underground lab. Mom and Dad had been there since early that morning, working on a big project. They were super-genius-scientists for B.R.A.I.N., a super-villain-fighting group. That meant they spent a lot of time working on big projects.

"Whoa!" Ellie exclaimed. She skidded to a stop at the doorway. Looking up, her eyes grew huge. She was standing inside a huge shadow. Mom and Dad's new project wasn't just big — it was GIANT!

A robot towered overhead. It had a large, round tummy and oversized arms and legs. It also had spotlights for eyes. Ears that looked like satellite dishes stuck out of its enormous head. It sort of looked like an overstuffed teddy bear, without the fluff.

Just then Dad stepped out from behind the robot's leg. "What do you think of our latest invention? Super, huh?"

Ellie surveyed the huge hunk of metal. Mom and Dad had made a lot of extraordinary stuff in the past. There was the Ultra TV, which showed Ellie's favorite shows in the galaxy. And how about the Ultra Sponge? It could soak up Ellie's biggest spills.

Their inventions came in all kinds of shapes and sizes. But none of them were this super sized.

"Why is the robot so big?" Ellie asked.

"I can answer that." Mom popped out of the robot's head. She was holding a screwdriver.

I wonder if the robot has a screw loose, Ellie thought with a giggle.

"Super-villains can be tricky to catch," Mom said. "Different tools might be needed for the job. So Dad and I put all those tools into one invention. Meet the ultimate villain-catching machine — the Ultra Giant!"

Ellie X-rayed the Ultra Giant's body. Inside, there were the usual things for catching super-villains — a catcher's mitt, a lasso, a vacuum cleaner, an anteater, and a Venus flytrap. But there were also unusual things, like a book of riddles, a too-tight sweater, catnip, and a bottle of fast-drying superglue.

"What's this tool for?" Ellie asked. She pointed to a large net in the giant's hand.

"It's a fishing net," Dad answered. "It can catch villains like Fish Face and the Big Ka-Tuna. But it can also snag villains on land."

He turned the giant's head around and pointed to two big circles. "The giant has eyes on the back of its head too. That way, no villain can hide. They're called See Everything Eyes — S.E.E., for short."

Ellie was getting super excited. The Ultra Giant could do lots of things — enough to keep her busy all day!

"Can you show me how it works?" she asked eagerly. "I can pretend to be a villain. How about the Cookie Crook?"

Imitating the thief, Ellie snuck behind the giant and snatched an apple off Mom's desk. The giant's S.E.E. spotted her, but it didn't move one metal muscle.

"Sorry, honey," Dad answered. He took the apple from Ellie. "The Ultra Giant isn't working yet. To finish such a big invention, we'll need more time."

Ellie was disappointed. Even the Ultra Giant couldn't save her from Saturdoom. But maybe her parents could still help.

"Do you want to take a break and play?" she asked. "Hannah can't come over, and I'm super lonely."

"Not right now," Dad said gently.

"Awww! But you've been working the whole day!" Ellie complained.

Mom climbed down. "Count me in for a game later. First, I need to untangle some robot insides." She popped the giant's stomach like a trunk. Out fell a mishmash of mixed-up wires. "You can help if you want."

That sounded as fun as fighting alien blobs — again.

"Nah," Ellie replied.

"I know!" Mom said. "While you wait, you can clean your room."

NOOO! That was worse than Ellie could have imagined. Her mom was unleashing the forces of Choredom on *her*!

"Do I have to?" Ellie asked with a groan.

Mom nodded. "If I didn't know better, I'd say your room had been hit by a torpedo. But there's a way to make the job easier." She pointed to a flashlight-looking gadget on her desk. "Use the Ultra Animator."

Ellie picked up the Ultra Animator. It was an older invention, so she already knew how it worked. It had two switches: ANIMATE and REVERSE. By aiming it at something and flipping the switch to ANIMATE, she could bring that object to life. By switching it to REVERSE, she could make the object normal again.

If I have to clean my room, at least I can make my stuff put itself away, Ellie thought.

Dragging her feet, Ellie trudged out the door. "When you're ready to play, you can find me upstairs!" she called to her parents. "Just look for the loneliest super kid in the world."

CHAPTER 2

Ruff!

In her room, Ellie held out the Ultra Animator. Then she stared down the piles of clothes, comic books, and other clutter.

"All right, Choredom," she said. "You might think I, Ellie Ultra, am no match for a messy room, but I'll prove I'm the queen of clean."

Click! Ellie flipped the animator's switch to ANIMATE. Out blasted a green ray. It fired on a pair of pajama pants.

The pants sat upright. They twitched. They turned. Then they went skipping off her bed.

When the pants hopped into Ellie's laundry basket, she switched the animator to REVERSE. She zapped them with a red ray, and they stopped moving.

"With the Ultra Animator, cleaning is a snap," she said. "Or, I *should* say, a zap!"

Ellie took aim at the rest of the mess. She animated her Butterfly Girl action figure. It went fluttering back into her toy chest. She animated her piggy bank. It wiggled across the floor and hopped onto her bookshelf.

Aiming the Ultra Animator at her desk, Ellie zapped her entire collection of Cupcake Friends pencil toppers. Then she opened the desk drawer. In went Vanilla, Sprinkles, Red Velvet, and Carrot Cake.

"In you go, Cookies and Cream," Ellie said as the last one hopped inside. She hit REVERSE and gave them a blast with the ray. Then she pushed the drawer closed.

After a few more blasts, the room was spotless.

Ellie flopped down on her bed to read. She might have defeated her chores, but she still had to get through the lonely hours of Saturdoom. Escaping into a comic book seemed like the only way.

"Now, where is *Princess Power, Protector of Sparkle Kingdom: Tiara of Truth*?" Ellie muttered. She looked for her comic under her blanket. It had been there before she'd started playing cards.

Checking behind her pillow, Ellie spotted her stuffed dog. "Super Fluffy!" she gasped. She swept him up and smoothed his shaggy mop of white hair.

If ever there was a super companion, it was Super Fluffy. He'd been at Ellie's side since she was a baby.

He had joined Ellie when she took her first steps and flew out of her crib. He had helped Ellie fight her first villain — a bad dream. When Ellie had saved her school on her first day, Super Fluffy had been at the celebration — along with Mom, Dad, the mayor, and the citizens of Winkopolis.

Ellie looked into the stuffed dog's big, round eyes. "I wish you were real," she said as he stared back blankly. "If you could play, I'd never be lonely."

Suddenly — *POW!* — a super idea struck Ellie's brain. She could use the Ultra Animator to bring Super Fluffy to life! It had worked on everything else in her room!

After clearing a spot on her bed, Ellie plunked down her furry target. "Here it goes," she said. She took aim with the Ultra Animator. Holding her breath, she flicked the switch to ANIMATE.

ZAP! A burst of green hit Super Fluffy square on the nose.

The room was silent.

Ellie listened closely, waiting for him to speak. For a long moment, her super ears picked up only the sounds of an ant crawling behind the bookshelf, until . . .

"Ruff!"

Next thing Ellie knew, she was getting drenched in doggy drool. "Super Fluffy!" she cheered as he covered her in wet kisses. "You're alive!"

With a lively pounce, Super Fluffy leaped to the floor. He stuck out his paws and stretched a long, waking-up stretch. Then he went sniffing around the room.

Ellie double-blinked. She couldn't believe her eyes. Her stuffed-with-fluff animal was a dog — a tail-stretching, room-sniffing, face-licking dog!

Super Fluffy sneezed at some scented markers. When he got to Ellie's backpack, he dug his nose into the pocket. Then he pulled out a tennis ball, trotted over, and dropped the ball at Ellie's feet.

Ellie picked up the ball curiously. "Are you trying to tell me something?" she asked.

Super Fluffy wagged his tail with excitement.

"Hmm . . ." Ellie wondered what he wanted to say. Usually, she used her brainpower to read somebody's mind. But that trick didn't work on animals. It looked like she'd have to use another super skill and guess.

"Does the evil super-villain Finders Keepers want a tennis ball for his collection?" she asked. Finders Keepers was famous for snatching things around Winkopolis. He added them to his Mine-All-Mine Gallery.

Super Fluffy's tail drooped.

"Okay, wrong guess. Let me try again." Ellie thought hard. Her eyebrows squeezed together and then shot up. "Oh, no! Is the ball really a spaceship from Planet Sphere? I hope it's not here to invade Winkopolis!"

Super Fluffy's ears flattened, and he let out a whimper.

Ellie bit her lip. The ball wasn't a villain's prized collectible or a UIO — unidentified invading object. Then what was Super Fluffy trying to tell her?

Super Fluffy jumped up and snatched the ball out of Ellie's hand. He tossed it into the air and chased after it as it bounced across the floor.

He sure is in a playful mood, Ellie thought.

"Oh, I know!" she suddenly realized. "You want to play! Am I right?"

"Ruff!" Super Fluffy snapped up the ball and wagged his tail happily.

Ellie left the animator on her bed and flew to the door. "That's exactly what I wanted to do," she said. "Super minds think alike!"

CHAPTER 3

Smarty Paws

The screen door banged shut as Ellie, followed by her four-legged friend, bounded into the backyard. Her cape rippling in the wind, she breathed in the day. Squirrels chittered in the treetops. Birds glided from branch to branch. A breeze sailed coolly through the warm sunshine. It was perfect for having fun with somebody, and who better than Super Fluffy? Thanks to him, Ellie could say so long to Saturdoom. Saturday was Satur*play*!

"Let's play fetch!" Ellie exclaimed. "I'll throw the ball, then you catch it and bring it back to me. Understand?"

"Ruff!" Super Fluffy answered.

Ellie's arm swung back. She lobbed the ball across the yard.

Quicker than a dog could scratch a flea, Super Fluffy snapped up the ball, dropped it at Ellie's feet, and waited patiently for the next throw.

Ellie threw the ball a few more times, and each time, Super Fluffy brought it back lickety-splickety.

"Wow, you're good at this game!" Ellie said. "I'm going to throw extra hard this time, so watch carefully." Her arm whirled around like a Ferris wheel and sent the ball soaring. It tore through the air, startling a flock of pigeons. After kissing a cloud, it fell onto the rooftop and rolled into the gutter.

Super Fluffy was already sitting attentively at the downspout. When the ball shot out, he caught it and trotted back to Ellie.

What a super-smart dog! Ellie thought as Super Fluffy sniffed a caterpillar. He knew exactly where the ball would end up!

Ellie gave the pup's ears a friendly scratch. "If you can fetch, I bet you can do other things. How about we find out?"

"Ruff!" Super Fluffy agreed.

"Let's start with some easy tricks," Ellie said. "Sit."

Super Fluffy was already sitting.

"Oops! I mean, shake hands."

Super Fluffy lifted his paw, and Ellie shook it kindly.

"Beg."

Super Fluffy whimpered. He looked up at Ellie with the sweetest pair of puppy-dog eyes she had ever seen.

"Adorable!" Ellie cried. "How could anybody say no to that face?"

It looked like those tricks were too easy. Flexing her brainpower, Ellie came up with some trickier things. "Can you walk on two legs?"

On his hind legs, Super Fluffy marched forward, then backward.

"Speak?"

"Ruff!" Super Fluffy barked.

Ellie guessed that meant hello — close enough. "Okay, Smarty Paws," she said, rubbing her hands together. She was going to give him the trickiest trick of all. "Can you pat your head and rub your tummy — *and* stick out your tongue — at the same time?"

With his tongue hanging out, Super Fluffy patted his head with one paw and rubbed his tummy with the other. He'd learned the trick lickety-split!

Ellie's jaw dropped as the dog bowed. Not even Mom and Dad could do that, and they could make a spotted zebra.

Super Fluffy amazed Ellie with some more tricks. Then they went back to playing fetch, which he was expert at. After Super Fluffy had retrieved the ball with his eyes closed, Ellie heard a scuffling sound. Suddenly a voice yelled, "Help!"

Ellie immediately shot into the air and surveyed the neighborhood.

Outside Hole-in-One Donut Shop, a lady was waving wildly. "My purse! My purse!" she cried. "That thief stole my purse!" She pointed down the street, where a man was running away with a yellow bag.

Holey glazed donut! Ellie thought. Someone needed her help!

Faster than you could eat a Long John, Ellie sprang into action. She soared to the top of the shop and plucked off the giant donut-shaped sign. Flying up from behind the thief, Ellie threw down the sign.

"Gotcha!" she said, catching him in the middle. He wiggled and squiggled, but the donut hole held him tightly.

With the thief in the donut's clutches, Ellie reached for the lady's purse. But it was gone!

"It was here a minute ago," Ellie muttered. She looked around on the sidewalk.

"Ruff!" At Ellie's side, Super Fluffy held up the purse. Without a second glance, he raced over and returned it to the lady.

Ellie was wowed. That dog was super great at a lot of things, but fetching topped them all!

CHAPTER 4

Doomsday

After the two heroes had dropped off the thief at the police station and brought the sign back to the donut shop, they returned home. Ellie sat on her bed, munching on a donut. Playing had made her tired. Well, that and saving the day.

"Time for a CBB," Ellie said. "A Comic Book Break!" She grabbed *Ice Boy's Day of Doom!* On the cover, her favorite frozen hero battled Doomsday, the trickiest villain in the entire comic book universe!

Doomsday, like any villain, had a no-good mission — he wanted to fill the day with doom and gloom. To do that, he played downright dirty tricks. He signed each trick with a frown that matched the ones on his frowny-faced suit.

"Poor Ice Boy!" Ellie said, scanning the pages. "First, Doomsday turns off his alarm clock. Next, he draws frowns all over Ice Boy's homework. And then he ties Ice Boy's shoelaces into a big knot. Untying a knot is impossible — super strength or no super strength!"

Ellie kept reading. Ice Boy caught Doomsday in the end, but he decided to let him go after Doomsday promised to fix everything. Sure enough, Doomsday's promise was a trick, and that villain got away!

All of a sudden something tugged on Ellie's cape. She peeked over her comic.

"Ruff, ruff!" Super Fluffy was holding Queen Bee's broken scepter. Queen Bee had used the scepter to rule Ellie's school — at least until Ellie's muscle power had snapped it in two. The puppy bounced around Ellie, nudging her with his nose and wagging his happy tail.

"You want to play, don't you?" Ellie asked with a giggle. "How about we make a deal? I'll play fetch, but only if I can read and relax too. Can we shake on that?"

Super Fluffy tilted his head thoughtfully. After a moment, he lifted his paw and shook Ellie's hand in agreement.

Lounging behind her comic book, Ellie threw the scepter across the room. Super Fluffy brought it back and waited to fetch all over again.

Throw. Fetch. Throw. Fetch. Fetching never seemed to get old for Super Fluffy!

On the fourth throw, the scepter landed in a heap of stuffed animals. Super Fluffy flew into the heap. Seconds later, he burst out triumphantly. With a terrific leap, he pounced onto Ellie's bed, landing on the animator.

Click! The switch flipped to ANIMATE.

Ellie looked up just in time to see green animation particles heading straight for her. "EEEK!" she shrieked. Quicker than the Grim Sweeper's broom, she swept up the comic book and ducked.

The green ray struck Doomsday's picture.

Ellie's heart started beating super fast. At any moment, Doomsday would step off the cover, on a mission to spread gloom throughout Winkopolis. His pranks would wipe everyone's smiles clean off!

I'll stop that! Ellie thought. She grabbed the Ultra Animator and pointed it directly at the super-villain's picture. Any sign of villainous life — a stuck-out tongue, two thumbs down, the stink eye — and she would blast him with the anti-animating ray.

But nothing happened.

Ellie waited and waited — but still nothing.

"That's weird," she said. "Doomsday should've come alive by now." Ellie eyeballed the Ultra Animator. "Maybe the animator's run out of juice."

Super Fluffy hid under Ellie's blanket. He wasn't so sure Ellie was right.

Just then, there was a knock at the bedroom door. "Ellie?"

Ellie almost shot through the ceiling. The possibility of unleashing a comic book super-villain had made her jumpy. Thankfully, it was only Mom.

"Dad and I need some things for the Ultra Giant," Mom called through the door. "We're going to the Hardware Horse. Want to come along?"

The Hardware Horse was a huge tool store. It had every kind of bolt and nail, so it was Mom and Dad's go-to place for gadget parts. Ellie liked going to play Spot Hardy. Hardy was a plush horse that was hidden somewhere in the store. If you found Hardy, you got a prize.

"Sure!" Ellie replied. "This time, I won't use my X-ray vision to spot Hardy. Promise!"

"Great," Mom said. "Come downstairs when you're ready."

As Mom's footsteps faded down the hallway, Ellie's nerves settled. Doomsday was still on the comic book cover. Winkopolis, as she knew it, wasn't toast.

Ellie kneeled down beside Super Fluffy, who was trembling under the covers. "It's all right, Fluffster," she said. "You don't need to worry about that super-villain. Just stay put until I'm back, and be a good dog. Okay?"

Super Fluffy whimpered.

Before leaving her room, Ellie grabbed the Ultra Animator. "I better put the animator away. Don't want any trouble while I'm gone!"

CHAPTER 5

An Ultra Mess

"Lug nuts!"

"Wingnuts!"

"Eye bolts!"

"Hook bolts!"

"Pile drivers!"

"Screwdrivers!"

At the Hardware Horse, Ellie listened as her parents went gaga over gadget stuff. No doubt about it — the hardware store was a super-genius scientist's paradise.

Finding things for the Ultra Giant was fun for Mom and Dad. But spotting Hardy, the store's plush horse, was way more fun. Ellie always got a different prize. Last week, it had been a stick-on mustache. The week before that, it had been a twisty straw.

But today Ellie wasn't so lucky. It was time to check out, and she still hadn't seen Hardy anywhere.

"Did you find everything you need?" the cashier asked as Ellie peeked behind the magazine rack.

Nothing!

"I didn't see . . ." Ellie looked up at the cashier. "Hardy!" The horse was sticking out of the cashier's apron!

"Here's your prize." The cashier handed over a small, squishy soccer ball. It looked like a perfect toy for playing fetch.

I know who will love this, Ellie thought. *Super Fetcher!*

* * *

When they got back home, Ellie helped bring everything inside, burrowed like the Mad Gopher through some wingnuts, and pulled out her prize soccer ball. She couldn't wait to show Super Fluffy. No doubt she'd be in for another lickfest!

All of a sudden her stomach rumbled like thunder.

"Dinner will be ready soon," Mom said. "I'm using the Ultra Meal-O-Matic. Cooks meals in three minutes — guaranteed!"

"Thanks, Mom!" Ellie said. She raced upstairs, opened her bedroom door, and nearly toppled over.

There was no tail wagging. There was no drooling doggy face. There was only her room, which — once the capital of Clean — was now Messville, USA. Clothes were piled high and turned inside out. On the wall, artwork was hanging this way, that way, and the other way. And every single one of Ellie's Cupcake Friends pencil toppers — which she'd carefully stowed in her desk — lay scattered across the floor.

Ellie plucked the Caramel Apple topper off her rug. Even an atomic torpedo couldn't make this mess! What had happened?

"Ruff!" Super Fluffy barked on Ellie's bed. Scattered around him was *Ice Boy's Day of Doom!* — ripped into pieces! He picked up part of the cover and jumped up and down.

"My comic book!" Ellie cried. It looked like it'd survived an attack from a ninja. Or a shark. Or a ninja shark. Super Fluffy must've gotten bored while

she was away. He'd turned her room into his very own pooch playground!

"Look at what you've done!" Ellie said with a frown. "This place is messier than a pigsty. It's even worse than Hogsbreath's lair, and that villain's a real pig. How am I going to clean everything up?"

Super Fluffy looked at Ellie sadly and dropped the shredded paper. With his tail between his legs, he retreated under Ellie's blanket.

Ellie sighed. Super Fluffy knew a lot of tricks. But he needed to learn one more — how to behave!

Just then, the door opened. "Dinner's ready —" Mom stopped short at the sight of Ellie's room. "This is a nuclear disaster!"

Uh-oh. Mom was talking like a scientist. That only happened when she was doing an experiment. Or if she was mad.

"I can explain —" Ellie started to say.

But Mom shook her head and held up her hand. "I'm not listening to any explanation right now. I asked you to clean up, and you didn't. In fact, your room is messier than before! After you've picked up everything, come down and eat." She marched out and pulled the door closed.

Ellie felt a knot in her stomach as big as the one in Ice Boy's shoelaces. Mom thought Ellie, superhero crime-fighter and all-around good kid, had created an ultra mess!

As the knot in Ellie's stomach tightened, Super Fluffy poked his nose out of the blanket. He jumped down and walked over to the topsy-turvy pictures on Ellie's wall. Reaching up, he nudged a picture, straightening it out. He straightened another picture. Then another.

Super Fluffy was cleaning up! Maybe he was trying to say sorry, and if that was the case, how could Ellie stay mad?

"Do you want to help me clean?" she asked. "Together, we can get the job done in no time."

"Ruff!" Super Fluffy agreed.

The duo got to work. They fixed the rest of Ellie's pictures. Then they turned her clothes right side out and put them back into her closet. Next, Ellie got her wastebasket, and Super Fluffy dropped the pieces of her comic book inside. She didn't want to throw away her comic, but even the Ultra Puzzle Solver couldn't put all those pieces back together.

At last, they gathered her Cupcake Friends pencil toppers. As Ellie dropped them into her drawer, she realized something. "I'm missing one," she said, counting her collection. "Where's Pumpkin?"

Super Fluffy threw his nose into the air and sniffed around. A moment later, he shot off like a boomerang, flying in and out of her closet.

Ellie held out her hand, and Super Fluffy placed the little orange cupcake inside. "Great work!" she cheered.

When the room was clean — again — Ellie bent over and gave Super Fluffy a thank-you pat. "You make a good partner, you know that? I bet you do since you're so smart." She held out the soccer ball prize. "This is for you."

"Ruff, ruff!" Super Fluffy leaped into the air happily. He grabbed the ball out of Ellie's hand and tossed it back and forth.

Ellie grinned while he played. She was glad to have Super Fluffy's company. Sure, he could make mistakes. But he was still a super companion. He had put a smile on Ellie's frowny-face day. With him to play with, tomorrow was sure to be all smiles too!

CHAPTER 6

Fetch That Villain!

The next morning, Ellie smiled brightly as she bounced into the kitchen. The day had gotten off to a great start. She had already tossed around the soccer ball with Super Fluffy. Before that, he'd curled up on her lap while she'd read *Ice Boy Chills Out*. And before that, they'd played Cookie Crook versus Ellie Ultra.

Having fun had worked up her super appetite. She reached over her parents and grabbed a waffle. Mom and Dad didn't even seem to notice. They were too busy staring at the Ultra TV and frowning.

"What's wrong?" Ellie asked, noticing their serious faces.

Mom pointed at the TV. "Looks like there's trouble in Winkopolis."

Trouble? Ellie thought. That couldn't be good. She chewed quietly as the reporter talked on the screen:

"Pranks are popping up everywhere, spreading frowns around the city. Street signs are spelled backward. Birdbaths are filled with rubber duckies. Coins are glued to sidewalks. Each prank is signed with a frowny face . . ."

A frowny face? Ellie's appetite disappeared faster than the evil super-villain Chameleon.

"Sounds like it's the work of a super-villain," Dad said. "But who's the villain?"

"Let's see . . ." Mom pulled out her Ultra Smartphone and checked B.R.A.I.N.'s website. It listed every evildoer from A to Z. "It could be April Fools. But she only strikes on the first day of April. It could also be the Bad Luck Leprechaun, but his tricks are marked with a three-leaf clover." She put away her phone and shrugged. "It's probably just a practical joker."

"What do you think, Ellie? Ellie . . . ?" Dad looked over, but he only saw waffle crumbs.

Fast as her super feet could carry her, Ellie raced to her room. She dumped out her wastebasket, grabbed the ripped-up pieces of *Ice Boy's Day of Doom!,* and assembled the cover as best as she could.

When the last piece was in place, Ellie gasped. Doomsday's picture was gone. In its place was a frowny face!

"Doomsday's alive!" Ellie exclaimed.

"Ruff, ruff!" Super Fluffy barked. He picked up one of the pieces and raced around her room, stopping at her pictures, then her closet.

Super Fluffy hadn't messed everything up, Ellie realized. Doomsday had!

Playing the ultimate prank, Doomsday had pretended the animator didn't work. That way, Ellie wouldn't zap him with the reverse ray. When the coast was clear, he'd stepped right off the cover and into the real world!

"I'm sorry, Fluffster," Ellie said. "You were trying to tell me that Doomsday escaped, and I didn't listen."

Just then, Mom called from downstairs. "Ellie! Dad and I are going back to the Hardware Horse. We're already out of screws for the Ultra Giant. Want to come and play Spot Hardy?"

"No, thanks!" Ellie answered. How could she look for a toy horse? She had a super-villain to find!

As soon as her parents left, Ellie zoomed into their lab. She knew exactly what she needed to stop Doomsday. "Super Fluffy, can you fetch the Ultra Animator?"

In the corner, Super Fluffy was sniffing the Ultra Giant. "Ruff!" He took off down a row of gizmos and doodads.

Ellie gazed up at the enormous robot. With all its villain-trapping tools, it was going to be a big help to B.R.A.I.N. one day. "If only you could help now," she said to the giant. "Doomsday's an extra-tricky villain, so he'll be extra tricky to catch. Too bad you're not working yet."

When Super Fluffy returned with the animator, Ellie planted her thumb on the REVERSE switch. "Let's go, Super Fluffy!" she said. "It's time to fetch a villain!"

CHAPTER 7

Frownopolis

The city water tower cast a dark shadow over the land. It no longer said *Winkopolis*. Instead, the *Wink* had been crossed out and replaced with different letters.

"*Frown*opolis," Ellie read. She narrowed her eyes at the new word. Next to the letters, there was Doomsday's signature frown. "Doomsday won't stop until he glooms everything up!"

Leaving the water tower behind, Ellie followed Super Fluffy. He was busy sniff-sniff-sniffing out Doomsday's trail of trickery. They passed the craft store, which was covered in frowny face stickers. They passed the bakery, where cookies were decorated with swirly frowns. They passed the post office, which was selling frowny-face stamps.

When they reached City Hall, Ellie pointed to the mayor's statue. "There's the sign from Hole-in-One Donut Shop!" It was spinning around the statue like a sugar-glazed Hula-Hoop.

The mayor stood on the building's front steps, frowning. Getting pranked had made *everybody* grouchy.

"My lunch!" grumped a woman who was picking plastic ants off her sandwich.

"My bike!" howled a boy whose tire was flat.

"My photos!" cried a photographer.

Ellie peeked at the images on the camera. Doomsday was in every picture, jumping out like the villainous Photo Bomber!

Super Fluffy and Ellie searched the entire city. They came across prank after prank. But no prankster!

Where is *that villain?* Ellie wondered.

Just then she heard grumblings outside the movie theater. A showing of *Ghost in the Funhouse* had just started, but moviegoers were already shuffling out.

Ellie flew up to a grumpy-looking girl. "Why are you leaving? The movie's not over."

"Somebody spoiled the ending," the girl said. "Turns out, there isn't any ghost. It's only a mouse!"

Ellie gritted her teeth in frustration. Rats! She was supposed to see that movie with Dad next week. So much for surprises!

"The same guy who spoiled the ending also talked through the whole movie," the girl said. "And he chewed his popcorn really loudly. As if that wasn't bad enough, he left his garbage everywhere!"

"Is he still in there?" Ellie asked hopefully.

The girl shook her head. "Nope. See?" She picked an empty popcorn box up off the ground. On the outside was Doomsday's signature frown. "He littered on his way out!" With an irritated sigh, the girl threw the box in the trash and stomped off.

Ellie scanned the horizon. Doomsday's pranks stretched as far and wide as she could see. There was no end in super sight. It seemed like the city's day of doom would go on forever!

"Poor Frown — I mean, *Wink*opolis," Ellie said, flopping down on a bench.

Super Fluffy tugged on her cape, trying to pull her out of her foul funk. He probably wanted to play.

"Not now, Fluffster," Ellie said.

He tugged again.

"No, Super Fluffy," she said, shooing him away. "We don't have time to play. Not with the ultimate bad-mood dude on the loose!"

But Super Fluffy would not give up. He tugged on her cape *again*.

"Super Fluffy, I said —" Looking down, Ellie noticed Super Fluffy was sitting next to another empty popcorn box. She spotted another box beyond that one and some cups beyond that. The garbage trailed down the road.

Suddenly Ellie understood. "It's a trail of Doomsday's trash!" she exclaimed. She leaped to her feet. "If we follow it, it'll lead us right to Doomsday. You figured that out, didn't you?"

"Ruff!" Super Fluffy barked. He stood tall, looking quite pleased with himself.

"Super Fluffy, you're a super genius!" Ellie cheered. "Let's go!"

CHAPTER 8

Trouble in Tiara Land

More pranks littered Doomsday's trash trail. Ellie and Super Fluffy went by a sewing store that had been yarn-bombed. They passed a pool that was filled with otters. They saw a pizza that was wearing a pepperoni frowny face. Finally they trailed back past the mayor's statue, which was now dressed in the mayor's underwear.

The mayor, not surprisingly, was still frowning.

Along the way, Ellie scowled as she picked up Doomsday's garbage. "I'm not sure which villain is worse," she said. "Doomsday or the Litter Bug."

Finally, the trail came to an end. Super Fluffy grabbed the last popcorn box. Then Ellie flew up and dropped everything into a passing recycling truck.

"*Doom Street*," Ellie said, reading the street sign. It should've said *Mood* not *Doom*, but thanks to Doomsday, all of the signs were spelled backward. "Hey, Hannah lives on this street."

Hannah! Ellie had been so busy searching for Doomsday that she'd completely forgotten about her best friend. Hannah was stuck at home helping with her sister's birthday party.

Hannah might not be chasing super-villains, Ellie thought, *but she's probably running around after candy fiends.* It was hard to say which was worse.

Just then a man dressed like a court jester stomped over. *Jingle jingle!* The bells on his shirt rang noisily. "I quit!" the jester cried.

Ellie was royally surprised. "What's the matter?"

"Someone ruined my show!" he replied. "During my juggling act, he threw rotten tomatoes at me. Then he took my face paint. Guess what he painted on everyone's faces? Frowns!" The jester yanked off his pointy hat. "I'll never perform at another birthday party!"

"Birthday party?" Ellie repeated.

The jester nodded. "It was a princess party, so I made balloon crowns. But he popped them all!"

As the jester jingled away, Ellie's super ears rang. Face-painted frowns? Popped balloon crowns?

"C'mon, Super Fluffy!" she said. "It sounds like there's trouble in Tiara Land!"

With her trusty sidekick at her heels, Ellie shot down the street to Hannah's house. Peeking into the backyard, Ellie cried, "Doomed dragons!"

Out back, where there should have been a pretty princess party, there was a flattened bouncy castle. There were frowny-faced finger sandwiches. There was a banner that read *Happy Sad Birthday Cece!* ☹ Worse yet, there were ten little girls who looked grumpier than the Troll King in *Princess Power, Protector of Sparkle Kingdom*. It was a fairy tale party gone way wrong.

"This birthday party is HORRIBLE!" Cece cried, the grumpiest of them all.

Spotting Ellie, Hannah ran over with a broken dragon piñata. "Ellie! I need your help. There's a party monster on the loose!" Super Fluffy poked his nose into the piñata and sniffed around. "Hey, did you get a dog? He looks a lot like your stuffed animal."

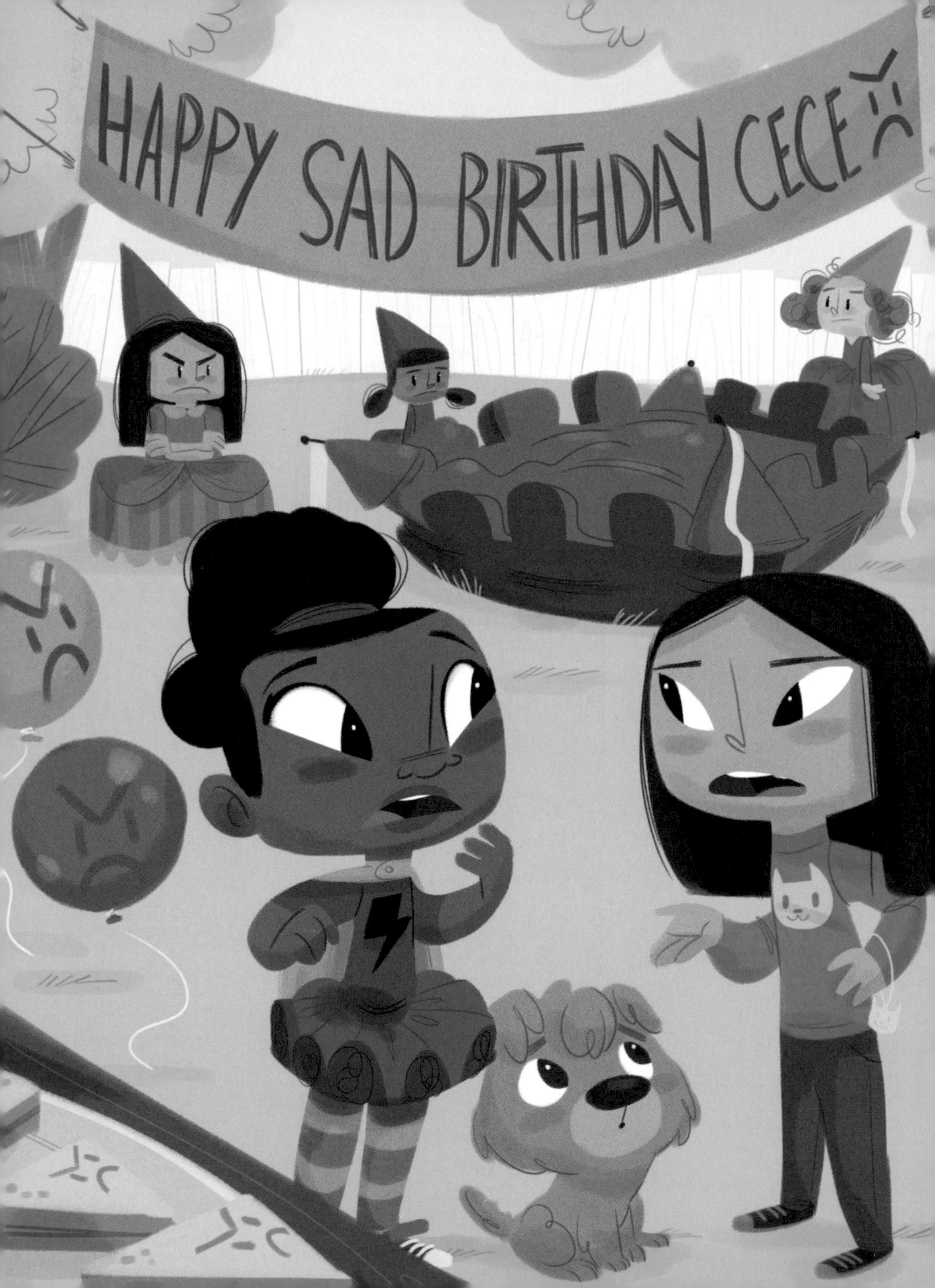
HAPPY SAD BIRTHDAY CECE

"Um, yep. I guess so," Ellie replied. Hannah didn't know Super Fluffy was *really* Super Fluffy!

"Anyway, it's a guest," Hannah went on. "He's taking the fun out of everything! He took all the piñata candy. You know what dropped out instead? Toothbrushes! And he put too many lemons in the lemonade. It's sour enough to make your toes curl!" Hannah pointed to a table that was full of goody bags. "Look! Now he's stuffing the goody bags with spelling tests!"

Ellie turned, and her face soured like a lemon with extra pucker-power. "Hannah, that's no guest," she said. "He's the Master of Misery. The Guru of Gloom. The Sultan of Sadness. Meet . . . Doomsday!"

CHAPTER 9

Day of Doom...
with Sprinkles

"Doomsday?" Hannah said nervously as they watched Doomsday grab another goody bag. He snapped it open and dropped a spelling test inside. "Is he a super-villain? Is a super-villain at my sister's birthday party?"

Ellie nodded. "I'm afraid so, but don't worry. I'll handle him. Besides, he's not as bad as Bovine the Bully. That villain can put you in a real *mooood!*"

"Okay . . . ," Hannah said, dumping the piñata in the trash. "Just keep him out of trouble while I'm gone. I have to find glue. Remember the crown party favors I had to make? Well, Doomsday picked all the gems off."

As Hannah walked into the house, Ellie set her super sights on Doomsday. He looked just like he did in her comic book, right down to his cloudy-gray hair and frowny-faced suit. He was a villain who could make all other villains cry for their mommies.

"This party is delightfully dull!" Doomsday cheered, filling the last goody bag. "Next, I'll open the presents and take out the toys. I can wrap up socks instead. That's sure to make the birthday girl frown!"

Slippery as a snake, the super-villain slid over to the pretty packages. Bows and bears and bubble-blowers flew into the yard. When he finished opening presents, Doomsday pulled a boring pair of plaid socks out of his pocket. Then he started to wrap them up.

Ellie bent down to Super Fluffy. "Wait here, okay? I'm going to sneak up on Doomsday and zap him with the Ultra Animator. We'll be back home before you know it!" With a blink, she made herself and the animator disappear.

Ellie's invisibility power made her a super sneaker-upper. Still, she couldn't be too noisy, or she'd give herself away. She carefully weaved around a play cell phone and an electric train set. "Eep!" she peeped, narrowly missing a bike horn.

Just another step and . . .

"The power's in YOU!"

Huh? Ellie lifted her foot. She'd stepped on a talking Princess Power doll!

"The power's in YOU! The power's in YOU!" The doll blabbed on and on, repeating Princess Power's

signature saying. It was going to blow Ellie's cover! Ellie fumbled fast for the OFF button. In her rush, she forgot to stay invisible.

"Ellie Ultra!" Doomsday hollered.

Rats! Ellie thought. *Caught!*

Doomsday smirked wickedly at Ellie. "Here to return me to the comic book, are you? Well, you'll have to catch me first. Until then . . . look out! Here comes a man-eating geranium!"

Ellie whipped around, but all she saw was an ordinary geranium in a flowerpot. When she turned back, Doomsday was gone. That trickster had tricked her!

"Nee-ner-nee! Can't catch me!" Doomsday reappeared at the bowling game across the backyard. He grabbed a bowling ball and let it fly down the lane. "STRIKE!" he shouted as the pins toppled.

"Game over, Doomsday!" Ellie yelled. "I'm sending you back to my comic book — where you belong!" She took aim with the Ultra Animator and flicked the REVERSE switch.

Doomsday ducked as anti-animating particles shot toward him. The ray missed, fizzling into a red burst. *FFZZT!*

Next the super-villain popped up at the punch bowl behind Ellie. "Nee-ner-nee!" he teased. "You see? I told you you couldn't catch me!"

This villain is trickier than a radioactive jumping bean! Ellie thought. Before she could zap him, he'd ducked out of sight. Keeping an eye on him was impossible!

On the prize table, there were frog prince squirt toys with funny puckering lips. Doomsday snaked over and sneered at the toys. "Ewww! Kissy faces!" Into the squirt holes, he put — what else — radioactive jumping beans.

BOING!

The frogs sprung into the air, carving a path of kissy-face destruction. They splashed in and out of the lemonade and knocked over the rest of the prizes.

Cece and her friends were standing around the bouncy castle. They had been playing inside before Doomsday let all the air out. Raining down, the frogs showered them with smooches.

"Kissing-frog attack!" Cece yelled. The girls drew their princess wands and swung at the puckering princes.

Ellie had to round up the frogs. But they were moving in opposite directions. Ellie couldn't be in two places at the same time — at least not without some help.

"Super Fluffy!" she shouted. "Let's fetch those frogs!"

Super Fluffy's ears perked. Like a furry firecracker, he shot across the yard and started snapping them up.

One, two, three, four . . .

Ellie grabbed a pillowcase from the Princess Pillow Sack Relay, and Super Fluffy dropped the frogs inside. Then they went after the rest.

Super Fluffy caught frogs on the left.

Five, six . . .

Ellie caught frogs on the right.

Seven, eight . . .

Cece held up her wand as the last two frogs charged. "Kiss me, and you'll be sorry!" she shouted.

Ellie swooped overhead and scooped them up. "Nine . . . TEN!" She tied the pillowcase tightly.

Just then, a voice called, "It's time for cake!"

The patio door opened, and Hannah's mom walked out with the birthday cake. It was the prettiest princess cake Ellie had ever seen! It had pink icing with white sprinkles and a bow that tied around the middle. On top, a fancy crown sparkled.

While everyone crowded around Hannah's mom, Doomsday peeked out from behind a bush. "I'll turn that princess cake into a royal disaster," he muttered, feasting his eyes on the frosted masterpiece.

Ellie gasped. If Doomsday ruined the cake, it'd be icing on the awful day! She had to stop him, but the Ultra Animator hadn't worked. What other invention could do the job? The Ultra Snapper-Upper? The Ultra Freezer? Maybe Super Fluffy would know!

"I need your help," Ellie whispered to her sidekick. "Fetch something that'll catch Doomsday. Nail clippers! A cheese grater! Anything!"

"Ruff, ruff!" Super Fluffy lunged at the animator and grabbed hold.

What in the universe . . . ? "No, Super Fluffy!" Ellie said, trying to pull it away. "The animator's no use! We need another invention!"

Super Fluffy tugged harder. His claws dug into the dirt as he tugged and tugged.

That dog was supposed to be a super genius. Why didn't he understand? "Super Fluffy, let go!" Ellie pleaded. "The animator's as useful as a robot without wires!"

With a mighty jerk, Super Fluffy yanked the Ultra Animator away. He raced out of the gate and disappeared.

Ellie's stomach twisted and turned. No ifs. No buts. No robot guts. She couldn't save the birthday party. Tiara Land was doomed.

CHAPTER 10

The Ultra Giant

"Before we eat, let's wash our hands," Hannah's mom announced.

Cece and her friends hurried away from the patio table and followed her inside. The cake was left behind, sparkling like a polished jewel. It dulled as Doomsday's shadow moved in.

"I'll turn this cake into my very own mess-terpiece!" he declared. "It'll have the works: old slippers, rotten eggs, cooties, extra-tangy barbeque sauce, and of course, my signature . . . A FROWN!"

Around the corner, Ellie listened helplessly. Her super best dog friend had run away. She was stuck facing the comic book world's worst villain alone. Even worse, that villain was planning a cake catastrophe!

"Now, for my first ingredient . . . an old slipper!" Doomsday pulled a slipper with shriveled up Odor-Eaters out of his jacket. But suddenly . . . *SNAP!* A lasso flew overhead, snapping the slipper away.

"Hey! What's the big idea?" Doomsday demanded. He turned and looked up, up, up.

There, casting a shadow over Doomsday, the cake, and everything else, was the big idea. It stood strong with thick metal arms and legs and a belly like an overstuffed teddy's — minus the fluff. Spotlights glowed brightly from its eye sockets, while satellite ears swiveled around on top of its head.

Ellie gasped. It was the Ultra Giant!

"That's impossible!" Ellie exclaimed. "Mom and Dad haven't even finished it yet. How come it's working?"

"Ruff!" Super Fluffy raced out from behind the Ultra Giant. He was carrying the Ultra Animator in his teeth.

The animator! Ellie realized. Super Fluffy had used it to bring the robot to life. They'd needed an invention to catch Doomsday, so he'd fetched the ultimate villain-catching machine!

Super Fluffy dropped the animator at Ellie's feet. "Super thinking!" she cheered.

The giant slurped up the lasso like it was a spaghetti noodle. It spit out the slipper and glared at Doomsday, who stood front and center in its spotlights. A large, wiry ball slid out of the giant's robotic hand and unfolded into a fishing net.

Doomsday smirked as the net dangled above him. "Going fishing, Tin Can Man?" he taunted. "Well, you'd better keep your eyes peeled. I'm trickier than a trout!" With that, the super-villain ran off into the shadows of the backyard.

Using its spotlights, the giant illuminated every one of Doomsday's hiding spots. It spotted him under the birthday banner. It spotted him beside the punch bowl. It found him crouching behind a silly garden gnome. But each time, before the giant could throw its net, the villain ducked away.

Doomsday popped up at the bouncy castle. "Yoo-hoo! Over here!" He wiggled his butt and then leaped out of sight.

When the giant looked over, Doomsday reappeared behind its back. "That tin can can't spot me now," he whispered. "It's time to make my mess-terpiece!" He took another slipper out of his jacket and slipped quietly toward the cake.

Ellie watched as Doomsday closed in on the sweet treat. She opened her mouth to warn the giant when — *SPROING!* Its arm flipped backward, launching the net. *THWAP!* The net caught Doomsday!

How had the giant seen him? Confused, Ellie looked up and saw its See Everything Eyes — S.E.E. for short — staring out from the back of its head.

Eyes like that could help catch the Cookie Crook, Ellie thought. *He always strikes behind your back!*

Tangled in twine, Doomsday's arms and legs flailed wildly. "Let me out this instant!" he yelled. "I have more gloom to spread! Who will make caramel onions for Halloween? Who will dress like Bigfoot and scare the pants off everybody?"

As Doomsday squirmed like a squid, a catcher's mitt came out of the giant's belly button. It scooped the super-villain up, net and all.

"Way to bust that bad guy!" Ellie said. She flew up and gave the giant a very high high-five.

Just then, Hannah marched over angrily. "I can't find any more glue! How am I supposed to fix all those crowns?" She noticed the giant and stopped. "Ellie, what is *that*? Please tell me it's not another villain."

"It's the Ultra Giant," Ellie replied. "It *catches* villains. Doomsday wasn't being a good party guest, so my dog fetched the giant from my parents' lab. It caught Doomsday in that net, but it has other villain-catching tools. There's a vacuum cleaner and Venus flytrap. Oh, and an anteater!"

Hannah stared for a long time at the metal marvel. At last, she said, "The Ultra Giant has a lot of tools, huh? Do you think it has glue too?"

CHAPTER 11

Tricking a Trickster

The Ultra Giant had just what Hannah needed —
the bottle of fast-drying superglue! The crown party
favors were fixed in no time.

"Whew, you rescued me!" Hannah said, gathering
them up. "I can put these in the goody bags. Much
better than Doomsday's spelling tests." She turned to
Ellie. "Since you're done catching villains, want some
cake?"

Ellie shook her head. "Thanks, but I need to get the Ultra Giant home. My parents are shopping for robot parts. They won't be happy if the giant is missing when they get back. I've seen enough frowns for one day!"

"Okay," Hannah said. "Thanks for all your help. You really saved the day!"

Ellie waved goodbye and led Super Fluffy out of the fairy tale birthday party. The Ultra Giant, with Doomsday tossing in the net like a tuna fish, trailed behind them. All was happily ever after, with sprinkles.

On the way back from Hannah's, Ellie quickly cleaned up Doomsday's pranks. With Super Fluffy's help, she fixed the street signs so they weren't spelled backward. Then she took the otters out of the pool.

Soon, everyone was smiling again. Even the mayor looked relieved, especially after getting his

underwear back. It was a happy ending for Frown —
er — *Wink*opolis.

* * *

When they got home, Ellie flexed her muscle
power. "Okay, Super Fluffy," she said. She lifted
Doomsday out of the giant's net. "Bring Doomsday
upstairs, and make sure he stays put. I'll be there
soon. First, I have to return the Ultra Giant."

All was quiet in Mom and Dad's lab when Ellie
and the giant walked in. Nothing bubbled, smoked,
or self-destructed, which, for a super-genius scientist's
workshop, was odd. The only thing that stirred
was Cyclops the iguana. He peeked out of his tank
and straightened up when the giant walked past,
making himself appear taller. Then he returned to his
crossword puzzle.

Ellie figured the silence meant one of two
things — either her parents weren't back from their

shopping trip yet or they'd run out of ideas for a new invention.

She pressed a button on the Ultra Idea Maker, and out slid a slip of paper that read: *Ultra Voice Changer — an invention that can make you sound like different things, such as a kazoo or a Hawaiian monk seal.*

"The Ultra Idea Maker works fine," Ellie said. "So I guess that means Mom and Dad aren't home yet."

The giant came to rest in the same corner it had stood in before. Holding up the Ultra Animator, Ellie took aim. It was easy considering her target was enormous.

ZAP! The reverse ray hit the colossal contraption. Its spotlights flickered out. Its satellite ears stopped spinning. In seconds, the giant was back to being her parents' invention-in-progress.

Ellie lowered the animator with a satisfied sigh. "That takes care of the villain-catcher. Now, onto the villain!"

Leaping into the air, she flew upstairs. Doomsday was frowning when she entered the room. His cranky-pants mood matched his frowny-faced suit.

"Go chase your tail, Kibble Breath," the villain snapped at Super Fluffy. The pup growled at him like a super guard dog.

Doomsday quickly perked up when he realized Ellie was there. "So how's your day?" he asked kindly. "I hope it's looking up."

"How's my day? How's my *day*?" The corners of Ellie's mouth went south. "First, you atomic torpedoed my room, and my mom blamed me. Next, you turned my city into prank central. Then you almost ruined the birthday party of my best friend's sister. I'm having the worst day ever thanks to you!" She pointed to the ripped-up cover of her comic book. "And don't even get me started on my comic."

Doomsday simply smiled, waving Ellie's words away. "Oh, there's no need to be angry about that," he replied. "Tell you what. If you let me go, I promise to fix that unfortunate mishap. I'll make sure it's as good as new."

Ellie thought back to *Ice Boy's Day of Doom!*. In the comic book, Doomsday had promised he'd fix everything if Ice Boy set him free. But when Ice Boy let him go, Doomsday had escaped. And now the super-villain thought Ellie would fall for that same trick! But maybe she could out-trick the trickster.

"I'll set you free," Ellie said. "But before you put my comic back together, let me get all the pieces. Until then . . . look out! Here comes a man-eating Cupcake Friends pencil topper!"

Doomsday looked puzzled as Ellie motioned behind him. "A what?" he asked, turning around. "I don't see anything but a Princess Power poster —"

CLICK! Ellie switched the Ultra Animator to REVERSE. The red ray fired out, zapping Doomsday. He disappeared in a flash. The net that had caught him fell into a rumpled heap on the floor.

Ellie's heart raced as she ran to her comic book. She peered at the torn-up cover. There, smack in the middle, was Doomsday. The animator had returned him to the comic book world — for good!

"Phew!" Ellie sighed. "That takes care of the villain." She turned off the animator and set it down — far away from her comic. "I guess I won't need this anymore."

"Ruff, ruff!" Super Fluffy ran up with the soccer ball, clearly ready to play.

Ellie reached for the ball, when she suddenly realized something — Super Fluffy was *still* animated!

She looked down at her furry friend and smiled sweetly. "You rescued me from being lonely," she said. "I don't think any other stuffed animal can say that. But you're more than a stuffed animal. You're my friend."

Super Fluffy stared back as if he understood. He was a smart dog — a genius, in fact — that could save the day, just like Ellie.

He'd fit in perfectly around here, Ellie thought. *I just have to make Mom and Dad see what a super idea that is.*

CHAPTER 12

A Super Team

"On her trusty steed, Steel Blossom, Princess Power charged the troll army. Dodging gnarled teeth and spiked clubs, she rode fearlessly after the Tiara of Truth. It was Sparkle Kingdom's only hope!"

Ellie stopped reading and looked down. Beside her, Super Fluffy was curled up, sleeping soundly. Saving the day must've made him tired.

"I hope you dream of bones, not bad guys," she whispered.

As Ellie turned to the next page in *Princess Power, Protector of Sparkle Kingdom: Tiara of Truth*, Mom and Dad popped their heads in the doorway. They were carrying bags of supplies from the Hardware Horse.

"Hi, honey! We're home!" Mom said.

Ellie put down her comic book and sat up on her bed. She glanced around her room. "So, what do you think?" she asked her parents. "Pretty clean, huh?"

Mom nodded approvingly. "It's so clean I'd almost think the Grim Sweeper swept it with his Broom of Doom. That evildoer didn't show up while we were gone, did he?"

Ellie shook her head. Luckily, she'd only had one super-villain to deal with today.

"Oh, good." Raising an eyebrow, Mom noticed the fishing net on Ellie's floor. "Ellie, is that the fishing net we'd put in the Ultra Giant? You know you shouldn't play with the inventions when we're not home. Remember what happened with the Ultra ACHOO?"

"I remember," Ellie muttered. One time she'd tried the Ultra ACHOO while her parents were away. A feather had flown out of the machine and tickled her nose, making her sneeze for a week! "But I wasn't playing this time. I used the net to catch that prankster causing trouble around the city. It wasn't a practical joker after all. It was a super-villain named Doomsday. He came out of my comic book."

Mom cast a curious look at Dad. Dad cast a curious look at Mom.

"Anyway," Ellie continued, "I tried to catch him, but he kept getting away. Lucky for Winkopolis, the Ultra Giant had no trouble at all."

Dad scratched his head. "How did you make the giant work? It's not finished. In fact, Mom and I had to get more screws. We cleaned out the whole store!" He lifted a bulging bag.

"It wasn't me. Somebody else got the Ultra Giant working."

Just then, Super Fluffy stirred. Blinking awake, he saw Ellie's parents and jumped to his feet. "Ruff, ruff!" he greeted them, his happy tail flying.

"Super Fluffy? But how? Is that really —?" Mom and Dad could hardly speak as Super Fluffy ran up to them. He stopped at Mom, who was holding a bag of lug nuts, and sniffed the bag.

"It's Super Fluffy, all right," Ellie answered. "I was looking for someone to play with, so I used the Ultra Animator to turn him into a real dog. I thought he could keep me company. Everything was okay until the animator brought Doomsday to life too, but Super Fluffy took care of that villain. He animated the Ultra Giant."

"Now why didn't we think of that?" Dad asked. He looked in Mom's direction.

Mom just shrugged. Then she put down the bag and picked up Super Fluffy. "I notice you haven't turned Super Fluffy back into a stuffed animal," she said with a knowing smile. "Is there a reason why?"

This was Ellie's chance! She took a deep breath, the same kind of breath she took when gathering her super strength.

"I was lonely yesterday," she explained. "But after Super Fluffy came to life, that changed. He makes a great companion. He knows how to fight villains — real ones *and* comic book ones — and he plays fetch. He can even do tricks, like sit, speak, and shake hands. So, I was wondering . . . can I keep him this way?"

"I don't know, Ellie . . . ," Dad started to say.

"Oh, and he can beg!" Ellie added quickly. "Super Fluffy, show Mom and Dad!"

Gazing up at Ellie's parents, Super Fluffy whimpered. His eyes turned into warm, fuzzy balls of puppy-dog adorableness.

"Awwww . . . ," Mom and Dad said together. They exchanged a look, and Ellie crossed her fingers.

Finally, Mom let out a sigh. "How can we say no to that face? Okay, Super Fluffy can stay animated. But he's *your* dog, Ellie. That means you're responsible for taking care of him, along with doing chores, finishing homework, and fighting villains — real ones *and* comic book ones. Can you do all of that?"

With her super partner at her side? "Yes!" Ellie cheered, clapping excitedly.

Mom laughed as Super Fluffy licked her cheek. "I have an idea," she said, setting the puppy on Ellie's lap. "How about Dad and I take a break from working on the Ultra Giant, and we can all play a game. Does that sound good?"

But Ellie didn't answer. She was too busy giggling as Super Fluffy bounced around, tickling her with licky kisses. Mom and Dad smiled at each other, then gathered their supplies and headed out of the room.

"Just think, Fluffster," Ellie said when the dog had settled down. "Since you've been alive, we've taken on a thief, radioactive squirt toys, and a comic book villain. Loneliness too! We sure make a super team." She held out her hand. "What do you say? Are we teammates?"

"Ruff, ruff!" Super Fluffy barked, holding his paw out to Ellie.

As they shook hands, Ellie grew excited for tomorrow. Whatever the day would bring — a man-eating pickle, a zombie snowman — it would be no match for Ellie Ultra and Super Fluffy — together.

GLOSSARY

absorbent (ab-ZOR-buhnt) — something that soaks up liquid, such as a washcloth, towel, or sponge

archenemy (AHRCH-en-uh-mee) — someone's main enemy

atomic (uh-TOM-ik) — relating to, or concerned with atoms, atomic bombs, or nuclear energy

catastrophe (kuh-TASS-truh-fee) — a terrible and sudden disaster

colossal (kuh-LOSS-uhl) — extremely large

contraption (kuhn-TRAP-shuhn) — a strange or odd device or machine

extraordinary (ek-STROR-duh-ner-ee) — very unusual or remarkable

fiend (FEEND) — an evil or cruel person

invading (in-VEY-ding) — entering forcefully, like an enemy

marvel (MAR-vuhl) — something that causes a person to be filled with surprise and wonder

radioactive (ray-dee-oh-AK-tiv) — materials made up of atoms whose nuclei break down, giving off harmful radiation

unidentified (un-ahy-DEN-tuh-fahyd) — not able to be recognized or identified

villainous (VIL-uh-nuhs) — having a cruel, wicked, or evil nature and character

TALK ABOUT ELLIE!

1. Ellie is lonely at the beginning of this story. Look back at the text and talk about some of the ways she battled loneliness. What are some other things Ellie could have done? Then talk about some things you do when you're feeling lonely.

2. Super Fluffy is Ellie's super-special companion. He helps her catch villains. Talk about the other things he does that make him a special friend. Do you have any super-special friends? What makes them unique?

3. Super Fluffy's favorite game is fetch. What is your favorite game to play? Talk about why that game is your favorite.

EXPRESS YOURSELF!

1. Ellie's parents needed an invention that catches villains, so they created the Ultra Giant. Use your imagination and draw your own villain-trapping invention. Don't forget to name the invention and explain how it works!

2. Doomsday is a super-villain who spreads gloom and doom, making people grouchy. Luckily, there are ways to fight a bad mood. Write a paragraph about what you would do to cheer yourself up.

3. At the end of this story, Ellie is ready to take on the next villain with Super Fluffy. Use your imagination and write a story about Ellie's next crime-busting adventure. Who is the villain she faces? How does she defeat the evildoer?

ABOUT THE AUTHOR

Gina Bellisario is an ordinary grown-up who can do many extraordinary things. She can make things disappear, such as a cheeseburger or a grass stain. She can create a masterpiece out of glitter glue and shoelaces. She can even thwart a messy room with her super cleaning power! Gina lives in Park Ridge, Illinois, not too far from Winkopolis, with her husband and their super kids.

ABOUT THE ILLUSTRATOR

Jessika von Innerebner loves creating — especially when it inspires and empowers others to make the world a better place. She landed her first illustration job at the age of seventeen and hasn't looked back since. Jess is an illustrator who loves humor and heart and has colored her way through projects with Disney.com, Nickelodeon, Fisher-Price, and Atomic Cartoons, to name a few. In her spare moments, Jess can be found long-boarding, yoga-ing, dancing, adventuring to distant lands, and laughing with friends. She currently lives in sunny Kelowna, Canada.

CHECK OUT THE REST OF ELLIE'S EXTRAORDINARY ADVENTURES!

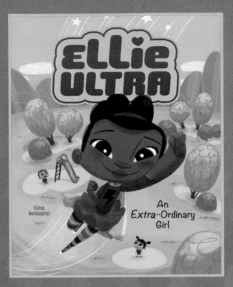

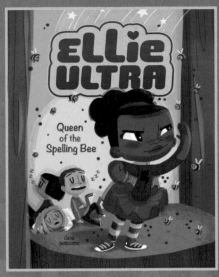

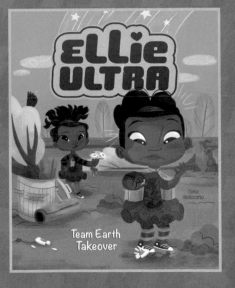

ONLY FROM CAPSTONE!